The Hat that Saved the World!

MEENA RAJPUT

JELLY BEAN BOOKS 2020

For my wonderful dad. Thank you for giving me the courage to reach my dreams x

Published by
Jelly Bean Books
Mackintosh House
136 Newport Road, Cardiff, CF24 1DJ
www.candyjarbooks.co.uk

Printed and bound in the UK by
Severn, Bristol Road, Gloucester, GL2 5EU

Our matching woolly hats are cool to wear.
They're green, warm and snappy.
In our hats, we've had adventures everywhere.
It makes us very happy!

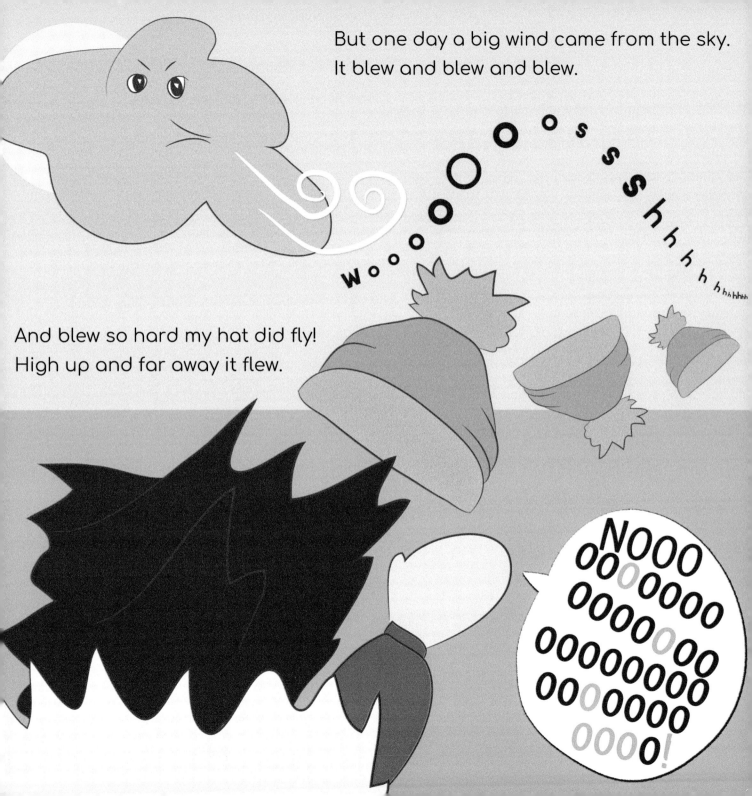

So sad I was.
I loved my hat!
But it was gone,
just like that!

Chidiya, the Arctic tern, flew and flew.
She flew so far, right out to sea.
Following clue after clue,
to find my hat for me!

CHIDIYA
MEANS 'BIRD' IN HINDI! SHE IS AN
ARCTIC TERN!
THEY HAVE THE LONGEST
MIGRATION OF ANY BIRD IN THE
WORLD! COOL!

As we started our journey, the baby narwhal did cry,
"Please help! Their noise is really hurting my head!"
"Sorry, we really can't stop!" I said with a sigh.
"And why don't you just swim away?" Bao said.

SINGLE USE PLASTIC

We sailed further on,
and a turtle screamed out.
"Please help!" he said.
"Save me from all this plastic!"

oWWW!

"But the whale is getting away,"
squawked Chidiya,
pointing to its spout.
"I'm sorry, little turtle!" I said.
"But if I lost my hat it would
be so very drastic!"

Further along still,
we saw little fishes
gasping for fresh air.
"Please help!" they cried.
"Free us from this sticky
icky oil spill!"

ICKY
STICKY
OIL
SPILL

But getting my hat back,
I thought, was just as fair!
"Someone will come by and help,"
I said. "Just wait and try to chill!"

The little whale seemed scared, lonely and sad.
"I'm sorry!" he said. "But I've lost my mum!
And I thought with this hat she'd find me.
Please don't be mad."
Poor little whale, we thought!
His story made us ever so glum.

"Never mind the hat, Mishi,
you can share mine!" said Bao.
"Let's help our friends!
Let's help Little Whale find his mum!"

"Little Whale," we said,
"We'll help you now!
And as for the hat,
you can keep that, little chum!"

Off Chidiya flew to look for Little Whale's mum.
She was in danger and scared and hurt!

Those horrible big people,
in the night they had come.
To take the whales when
they weren't alert!

Off we went to save Little Whale's mum!
"Stop hurting our friends,
it's really not fun!
Would you like it if we
did it to you?"

As we sailed back to the Arctic, we stopped to set the little fishes free.
"Stop spilling your sticky icky oil in our ocean!" we shouted.
"It's hurting our friends, can you really not see?"

We sailed further on, and stopped
to help the poor little turtle!
We swooped up all the horrible plastic,
and sent it back to the big people with
a message in a bottle:

...without all your **PLASTIC**, our ocean is **FANTASTIC!**

Yoink!!

Further along still, we set the shark and manta ray free.

NO BIG BAD FISHING NETS ALLOWED HERE!

"Fishing is not allowed in our ocean," we chanted. "Leave our friends to be happy in the sea!"

Our narwhal friends needed us too!
"Shhhhh," we told the big people.
"Your nasty noise maker is killing us
– do you really have no clue?"

But when we got to the Arctic,
Bao's house was melting away!
It was the big people **AGAIN**
who caused it,
by making our planet
get hotter every day!

OHHH NOOOOOOOOOOOOO!!

Don't worry my friends,
we built a new home for Bao!

PLEASE
WILL YOU
HELP US?

But soon,
they say,
that too will
melt away!
So please will
you help us,
right now?

BECOME A LITTLE WARRIOR!

Will you please write a letter to all the big people in charge? To say our world would be better if they treated it with much more love and care!

1. Parents, guardians, family, and friends; please help your Little Warriors send a letter or the postcard supplied in this book to their local politician, who should respond directly to any written mail. You can find your local politician's address online.
2. Help your Little Warriors share this story with their friends and family!
3. Help your Little Warriors inspire others by sharing their activism on social media! #LittleWarriors #TheHatThatSavedTheWorld

Hi, I'm Meena and I'm an activist! My own adventures have inspired me to write and illustrate stories for young children about the *magic of activism.*

It's up to us to make sure our little ones always feel empowered to protect the things they love, and to know that by working with their friends they can help to make a difference to our world!

As a British Indian woman, representation is also a really important part of my storytelling. It is crucial that our children of colour have access to role models they can relate to, and that they too are imagined by all of society as our future heroes and change-makers.

So parents and guardians, please help me to protect our children's futures and inspire them to become Little Warriors that take care of each other and our planet.

Meena